The Winter of Our Femininity

By Hellena Jane

Petrichor

PUBLISHING

The Winter of Our Femininity © 2020 by Petrichor Publishing

Cover designed by Madeleine Ismael

Petrichor Publishing
www.publishpetrichor.com

First Printing: December 2020

Petrichor Publishing
1604 Brookhaven Circle
Bedford, Texas
76022
United States of America

"What would happen if one woman told the truth about her life?
The world would split open."

– Muriel Rukeyser

PROLOGUE

The funeral is a steaming affair. The sun shines down in an undesirable way for such a sad occasion. Any other assembly of people would be happy, smiling with their faces tilted upwards to feel the gorgeous yellow warmth spread over them.

No one does that here, and our black clothing absorbs the heat. It makes sweat run down our backs, pooling in our seats. I stare at my black shoes; they have a scuff on them, probably from the pavement I had stumbled on walking here. I wish I could reach down and force it off with a rubbing of my fingers.

What is everyone thinking of me? I shouldn't have come here. Especially with a scuffed left shoe. *Who does she think she is?* they're thinking, *she didn't even know her.*

I want to address them and their stares. *I knew her*, I want to tell them. *In her death, I knew her better than all of you, you murderers.*

I see Lottie is here, her dress far too short for such an occasion. Her body is slumped on Ed's, his arms holding her body up. She looks as if she has not stopped crying; her eyes are bloodshot and her nose looks almost rubbed raw by the screwed up tissue she is holding in her hand. She looks like a mess. Good.

Ed looks as if he is doing better— in fact, I can tell he is. His jaw is set solid and tight, his mouth a fine line. He looks everywhere but the freshly dug grave. The air holds the smell of fresh dirt. The muscles in his arms look well-defined once again, like they did back in our first year of classes. He's been working out. Who can work out so quickly after the death of a loved one?

I wonder how he pictures her now... is she the pile of broken bones on the patio floor with a pool of blood growing around her? Or as the girl he used to fuck, slumped together in a small bathroom at parties? I think a lot about the moment he saw her, her blood slipping between the slates, washing the dirt away. His eyes were glossed over with some kind of knowledge. His jaw was locked, the same way it is now. *What do you know?*

He hadn't screamed the way I had, and I didn't even know her name. I hadn't touched her as he had. His life had been so mixed with hers. He didn't even cry.

Lottie had been different; she had tried to touch the body. She tried to hold it, like an actress selling the final scene in a Shakespearian tragedy. She made the whole thing harder to look at, and the paramedics and the police had to pull her away. She clawed at them. She had to warm her up, she told them. She was cold. She needed her.

The body was no longer the star of the show, it was Lottie. Once again she had solidified her status as a leading lady, as the body was whisked away.

Varjack had been a similar case, but he didn't turn up to his lectures for two weeks. When he did show up, it made me wish he had never come back. His clothes were crumpled, and to be near him was to smell a mix of urine and vodka. He mumbled his way through the slides, but collapsed in his seat halfway through, his tears choking him and making him cough. I didn't want to comfort him like the other girls in the class. I wanted him to feel what he had made her feel. But his tears didn't last long; he found a new girl soon after.

Today, he stands close to her. She whispers something to him, her long blonde hair swishing forward with her motions, capturing the light. She didn't care for where she was. His eyes gleam, her death means nothing would change for him. And he is here, I presume, to make sure her secrets she had threatened to spill would be buried with her.

The family stands close to the hole as her remains are lowered in. I close my eyes tight. I try to think of happy places, happy things, but only see her open eyes, so surprised with the pain of her fall. I see what her body must look like now, rotting and pale. Her eyes though... her eyes are still the same.

I hear someone let a sigh of relief out from behind me. I whip my head around but I can't tell who it was. I turn back as the family throws soil on the coffin.

I hear a whisper, meant to be quiet but loud enough for the second row to hear.

'I'm not sad she's dead.'

TWELVE HOURS

The decision to get up that morning felt completely natural. For some, she knew, it would be far too early. For some people out there (who she certainly did not know) it was far too late. She enjoyed waking to the confusion of last night.

The rain had once again begun to tap against her windows. The old capital of a forgotten empire had begun to beat like the heart of a lover. She wandered through her home, which looked like someone had been frantically searching for someone or something. Her drawers were open with small lace thongs pouring like a frozen waterfall; her jewellery was clumped together to feel the safety in their numbers; wine glasses stained with lipstick smudges lay overturned on most surfaces. She moved past it all without a care.

Her soft steps moved her to the bathroom, where she studied herself in the mirror. Although her face still contained the hauntings of last night, she was pretty. Pretty in the sense that she was rich, educated and saw the world much like a child. Her body was nothing revolutionary, and she hoped no one had written home about it.

She only really liked her eyes anyway. The green and blue tones of her eyes made her happy because they looked like jewellery boxes, and jewellery boxes always contained happiness. The strong eyebrows of her face framed high cheekbones, and a small smile scuttled across her face.

She splashed herself with icy water to tamp out the red-hot sleep. She wondered what men saw in her. What *one* man in particular saw in her. *It must be the soulfulness of my eyes*, she thought, tilting her head from one side to the other.

She enjoyed how her hair felt as it moved across the bareness of her back. *How wonderful*, she thought, *it is to be naked*. How utterly gorgeous it was to study the female form simply by waking up and looking in a mirror.

Did all women do this? she asked herself. *Am I the only one who dares to look upon their own beauty and not feel ashamed? Have no blood rise to my cheeks, no uncomfortable stones in my gut?* How gorgeous the feeling was, though she knew it would never last and that it would fade out into nothingness like the momentary, delicious taste of bubblegum.

Regrettably, she moved away from the mirror, bounced down the stairs in all her naked glory to make coffee and see if there was anything she could put in her empty, growling stomach. A girl had to eat. Once, she got so hungry, she arranged a date just to be taken out for dinner.

She ought to check the front door, and panic rose in her chest, just for a moment, until she pressed her hand against the cold metal, solid and unmoving. Locked. Relief filled her body like a shot of something alcoholic, warming up all the corners of her stomach. It can be as Fitzgerald once claimed: For a girl such as this, there's nothing better than to be a fool, a beautiful little fool.

She checked her phone. Varjack had texted, and what fills a girl more than food than the attention of a male? In fact, he had texted not once, but *three* times in a row. His attention, like a beam of light, came straight from the heavens and filled her up with glowing neon lust. She thought of him, thinking of herself as his blushing Lolita. She thought of his hands on her, she thought of the touch of his fingertips. She blushed and texted back one text longer than his three short ones. He read it, waited for only a couple pauses of his breath before replying. Her head spun out in thoughts of lust, and she began to decide what she should wear.

Ah to be young, to be stupid, and to be a girl with the world bowing down to you with every one of your gentle steps. She wondered what she would look like with wrinkles. She then decided she would kill herself before the skin covering her muscles and bones had a chance to lose its elasticity. *That will be my legacy,* she told herself. *I will be forever beautiful and young in my coffin.* What could be more haunting and darling than that?

The thoughts churned in her head like the swirling of ribbons at a maypole dance in the watery warmth of middle England as she ascends alone up the stairs. It felt so real to her, she could float off in her thoughts and be lost to the world of taste and colour. But she couldn't, because she had a date. A date with a real man. Tight around the maypole they go, as the smile on her face grew and grew.

Dear reader, you may wonder why this girl should matter to you. You might be saying, why should I, dear narrator, care what this child dressed in women's clothing does?

Well, my dear reader, this girl will soon be dead. If you had twelve hours left of life, what would you do? What mystic forces and players would you confront? But more importantly, *most* importantly, who would you be afraid of?

Though a dead girl's body does not move, does not speak or sigh or point— the dead tell their story, dear reader, if you look close enough.

ELEVEN HOURS

She stood uncomfortably, like some kind of magazine model, at the red door in a neighbourhood where she knew but only one person. The number of times she had driven past here, desperately hoping to catch a glimpse of him and desperately hoping to not see him, were uncountable.

Exactly how many times, she wondered, *had I stared up at the Victorian bay windows of the brown brick house? Filled with desperation, deeper than the ocean itself, to know what it would be like to look out of those windows instead of always looking in?*

Her fist gathered all the energy needed to make noise and signal to him that she had arrived. Something stopped her, though. There was a pit in her stomach and a storm gathered over her head. She could not tell if the static in the air excited her, or was a warning about the person who would be opening the door. Would this be the last time she ever knocked?

If I could stop this, do you not think I would, beloved reader?

Never mind now, as her fist made contact with the wood and she begged her heartbeat to slow, he opened the door.

She stepped into four cream-coloured walls, and once again was forced to drink him in. Her mind begged her imagination to forget the wrinkles around his eyes, the silver quality of his hair, the paleness of his skin. He bore no resemblance to the character she had given him the pet name of, and he did not make her feel like Audrey Hepburn.

But what did that matter? She could be Audrey in her own time, she could make herself feel like that. His attention made her

11

feel more like Marylin... oh, but how could she ever be Audrey when she had only lived like Marylin?

She sat down, and watched him watch her body move. She had chosen the right dress.

'How are you finding the class?' he asked her, and she could almost see the cogs move in his head as he wondered how many questions he had to ask until he could touch her. How much small talk would he have to deal with before he could take her upstairs? The answer, for Varjack, would always be too many questions, too much small talk.

'I like it,' she said, and he moved closer to her with every word. 'I think it's hard to watch you lecturing and know what you're like without clothes on,' she said as an afterthought. But it felt forced, uncomfortable, and sore. *I feel like a terrible actress*, she thought to herself. *He can see right through me.*

But, dear reader, he could not.

'This will have to be a quick one,' he said, lifting her hand to graze his lips, 'I have essays to mark.' He defined the look on her face as panic, so quickly he told her, 'Don't worry, this isn't going to change your grade.'

She let out a soft sigh. *Is he right?* she asked herself. *Do I do this for a good grade? Or do I love him? I wish I loved him.*

A pit opened up in her stomach as he held her hand and led her up the stairs. She wondered if he held the hand of his wife like this. Or did he value her body more, and therefore treated it with kindness in a way he never did with hers? She wanted to run, or better yet stay and tell him how she felt: the version of him that played over and over in her head was not the real him, that being touched by him felt like something so innately wrong it scared her.

Even as she walked up the stairs, she heard the living memory of his wife, a woman who was currently sitting outside. Who had watched a young girl enter her home and be greeted with a look on her husband's face that she had not seen in months. Our girl, with every breath, could almost feel the wife's heartbeat instead of her own. And with this, our girl almost understood now why their encounters always seemed fake and she never was able to enjoy them the way she pretends to.

She wanted to be spoken to and *heard*, for the first time. And maybe if he really listened, for the first time in his pig-brained life, he would do something right. But that, dear reader, is not our story. I am sorry to type out the truth, but it is what it is.

She noticed in his bedroom the copper frames that held pictures of his wife and family were turned away. Maybe he didn't want her to see the fake layers of his life. He didn't want the only true part of his love to see all the lies he had to live. For the first time since she had come inside the home, she kissed him with some pale imitation of real passion. The stubble of his chin moved under the softness of her palm. He undressed her hungrily, now wanting her.

She pushed him back, towards the bed. As she moved towards him, her eyes heated with something he wished was passion, and everything he liked about her vanished before him in the blink of an eye, a twitch of a curtain, the slowing of a car on the street outside, spying on a girl and a professor. She wished them both to be something they were not, and hoped that if she closed her eyes hard enough, it would be different.

Dear reader, there is a moment in every encounter like this where both parties are more in love with themselves than the other body on the sheet, and would rather be alone. But they cannot be alone. So, they are left here, in their eternal purgatory filled with only half-present love. The dread of being alone soaks into their bones. This was the feeling that will haunt them, follow behind them, until they push something into the open air in the hopes of becoming free again.

Dear reader, is this why she now lies cold with her organs donated to a body that knows love and passion so well? Could we assume, dearest reader, that the lack of love drives her to this tale's sorry end?

Just like that, the act was over. As it began, it ended with a kiss, but she still clung to him because he was the only thing there. All the static had departed from the air. *It's okay that I feel this way*, she told herself, because *everything once worth something is now nothing.*

She had somehow lost something to him once more. He felt as if he should send her away and get her back again, refilled with more beauty for him to eat up and take away from her. But he didn't believe he took it. In his mind, he gave beauty to her. He made her worth, and he could take it away too. He was a god over her body.

This thought made him wonder... was he only interested in her as it abused his powers? He shook the thought aside; all the great men of history have had young lovers, he told himself. He was in line with the greats now.

I can only imagine, dear reader, that as he stroked her hair as she rested on his chest, he wondered what it was like *inside* her head. He wondered what her brain looks like— the veins, the organs. He imagined what he might feel like if he wrapped her cooling body in the white bedsheets he had devoured her in. He imagined the colour of her blood, and he found himself filled with jealousy for the one who took her virginity. He felt green now, like Gatsby's light reaching for something he could never truly grasp. It didn't matter. He wanted to spill her blood to consume more of her.

Once more she kissed him, and he bit her lip hard enough to leave a red mark like the deep red wine on white carpet, letting any other man know— she was his.

He was pretending to enjoy this moment, with her head on his chest, but he could not. The head was heavy, his arm slowly turned numb from being underneath her body. She was as crumpled as the sheet they lay upon. The wet warmth of the bed had begun to grow cold and with its decrease in temperature, his desire for her cooled as well. He wanted her to leave. Leave him to his guilt of having her here. He faked a yawn and she looked up at him.

'Tired?' she asked, moving her head softly to the side. Her eyes were wide and trusting. It brought to mind the time as a child he had kicked the neighbour's puppy that had the same look in its eyes. Since then, dear reader, it is safe to say he has always enjoyed violence against the things he saw as most vulnerable in the world.

She started to move from the bed, releasing pins and needles throughout his arm. He rolled onto his side, and watched her dress somewhat frantically. Watched her body, without the rose coloured lenses of lust. He noticed her breasts, the right slightly bigger than the left. And stretch marks, white and gleaming against the skin of her hip bone. As she reached her arms up into her top he could see the small, short armpit hairs growing back in.

All this filled his mouth with a distaste for her. *How dare she not be perfect?* he thought. Her body, living and breathing and growing, would never be the perfect stillness he longed for. He sighed and wondered if there could be anyway he could make that dream of a perfectly still and steady girl come true to a girl he had only ever known to move.

He walked her down the stairs, thinking of how easily he could trip or push her. Watch her final twitches and the dark blood move slowly until all the air was filled with its metallic scent, and the dark wooden floor glossed with its burgundy brilliance. She would look like an offering to the gods, she would look pure like the statues of Mother Mary he had stared at so often growing up. They reach the bottom of the stairs and the moment passed; he cannot make her something more than she is now. The magic had worn off.

She turned and smiled softly at him. 'I guess I'll get going then,' she said, but there was an edge in her voice that made him suspect that she's upset. Why would she be upset? She loved to do this; he knew that much.

He didn't press it and stepped closer to her. Leaving a small kiss on her cheek, her breath smelled sour and he turned his face in distaste once more. She opened the door and the noise of the city once again fell into their ears. He grabbed her wrist, smiling at her.

'Stay safe out there,' he told her. She nodded and slipped through the gap in the door. He was once again alone.

Now, dear reader, as this man daydreams the breaking of a skull, a man who is haunted by the dreams of pooling blood, may I ask who you believe to be the killer?

NINE HOURS

As she left Varjack's house, the wind felt colder pressed against her skin, as if it had found its way between the thin layers of her clothing. Everything felt wrong. Her pants sat incorrectly between her legs, the sock on her left foot felt as if it was not on completely. She needed to undress and redress without the hungry eyes of a man on her.

But even if she did that, she would still feel strange. The pavement was too hard— life was too hard. She felt as if she had been pulled out of the box too soon, as if she wasn't ready for the sudden twists and twirls life could take.

However, it wasn't nighttime yet. The day was still long, filled with endless encounters and pointless conversations. Her eyes had begun to water at the thought of the numerous men who would speak to her, who would ask her how she was feeling but not care. There was no one— not one person— who could take away the powerful pushing waves of the something she was feeling. She was utterly and absolutely alone in an entirely overcrowded world. She thought about how to soothe herself, but felt only death would help.

She called a car, and it took her home. The driver earned himself five stars when he said nothing as she almost cried at the sight of a beautiful couple stopped at a red light. She couldn't decide which of the hand-holding couple she was more attracted to.

Don't you think it's odd, dear reader? The basic weaving of our lives with others? There was no reason for our dear sweet girl to know the man driving her home was, in fact, one of the most delightful men with the saddest life story. The tears you would cry while he spoke would taste much like powdered sugar, and the words that he would impart to her could stop the reason I am telling this story.

She and the driver moved through life like the silent stars, speaking nothing to each other and unable to stop the fearful fate which shone like the sun. If only we could reach out, touch fingertips, and know— we are not alone.

He stared at the girl through the mirror. He could see the perfect singular tear that rolled down her face, and he could see the earth-shattering pain that was in her eyes. *She was lost*, he told himself. *She was like a little boat in the stormy sea. I should say something.*

He opened his mouth, and I wish I could tell you that he was able to say something to her, to get her to talk through all the thoughts in her head and all the sadness in her bones. But, I have told you before, the most beloved reader of mine: I cannot change the truth.

The car pulled up outside her house. He cleared his throat to say something, and she took it to mean she should get out. He watched her get out and tried to convince himself that she would be just fine.

'Thank you,' she mumbled as she stumbled out of the car, slamming the door behind her. Even her home felt colder than she remembered, which simply came from the heating being switched off. The blue tones of the halls seemed to echo her own blues.

She decided there was nothing left to do but to bathe, hoping that would pull the odd feeling from her body. She felt as if she could fill the bathtub with her tears, like Alice. She feared if she started crying, she would not be able to stop. That she would drown in her own tears. She put it off. *Some things are best left for tomorrow*, she thought as she turned the hot tap.

Something about running water always reminded her of her mother. A woman who bathed more than anyone else she could think of. Bubble baths, bath bombs, salt baths, ice baths, even simple baths. Nothing but you and the water and any thought you had, which you could try and hold under the surface long enough for it to never breathe again.

As she undressed, she thought of the other ways to kill off her thoughts. Push them out a window, let the dark night take hold of them. *Would they float there?* she wondered, *or would they fall down and seep into the mind of someone else?*

She stepped into the bath; the water was so hot it brought another tear to her eye. *Good.* Burn him out of the memory of her skin. *Sterilization*, she thought, making herself chuckle. Purify the body before it can be sacrificed, like what they did to mummies to make them ready to enter the afterlife.

Now safe with her body trapped under the hot water, she began to count on her fingers the ways she could free herself from Varjack. She could threaten to tell his wife, his beautiful wife. She could tell the other faculty at the university, although she would have to remind them who she was, given that she never went in.

What would he do? Would he beg? She thought of how amazing it would be to see him beg. All the manliness she once found so attractive would seep from him and no longer would he scare her into anything.

The possibilities began to spin out of her mind like dancing ballerinas, twirling and spinning. She felt, for the first time in a while, like she had power again. She had forgotten, like most women do, how *fantastic* power tasted.

EIGHT HOURS

Now, dear reader, it is time for me to introduce the closest and most beloved friend of our girl. Some people say that those you surround yourself with are a better example of who you are. In my humble opinion, dear reader, this is wholly false and comparable to what comes out the back of a horse.

When in my youthful days, I was fortunate enough to be surrounded by smart, powerful women, whose minds could have fit in with all the great philosophers. But I, a fool, let them die off without ever genuinely *hearing* them. Nowadays, the person I speak to the most is the delivery guy. Friends are nothing more than furniture in our lives. Take it lightly, dear reader, there is trouble ahead.

We, unfortunately, come to meet one Miss Lottie MacNair. Her family came down from the highlands of Scotland in the seventeenth century to associate with the savage English and help them become civilised— like the Scottish, you see. They then tried to sue Shakespeare for defamation of character at the release of Macbeth.

Yes, her family came from an extensive line of men who defined themselves as important, and now that line had produced a girl who looked down on so many people it was impossible to see anything but her own nose. All that money had coupled with self-righteousness to make her see the world, and others, as something stuck to the bottom of her shoe.

Now let me introduce you to one Mister Edward White, on-again, off-again boyfriend of the witch MacNair. This is a boy, who like most boys of our generation, has made his style from gentrifying working-class charity shops. He claims not to be racist, but thinks he can say the 'N' word freely. He claims not to be sexist, yet believes the clothing on a body can communicate if its wearer wants sexual advances to be made (and often ignores if he thinks they communicate, 'no'). Dear reader, I am not lying when I say this: Ed is the epitome of all things wrong with our world.

Discussing such people as these two makes me sick. Some people in life are not human, but demons who feed on pretty, bright-souled people. Dear reader, I beg you, look away now and allow me to type no more. It is far too painful. You won't? Fine.

The phone rang out, its loud noise carried to the bathtub where our girl felt weightless. She allowed herself to close her eyes and feel the stress and the mess of the situations she got herself in float away. If only she would let it ring out, let the beep take it for her, and be alone with her thoughts. She could, for the first moment in her life, establish real contact with herself. Not in the understandings of beauty or all the labels she had been given her whole life— no, not that. An authentic and real moment. That could be enough.

But she heard the phone clearly, it rang out and broke her peace with a strong fist. She rose, letting the water run over her skin to splash upon the dark wood floor. She answered the phone just before the last ring.

'Hello?' she mumbled, holding the towel around herself tightly as if it were a second skin. Where was the girl from the morning who saw herself as the most perfectly formed being? She searched her mind for the glowing confidence that had bubbled like tonic water but found nothing, nothing at all.

'Where the hell have you *been*?' screeched Lottie. She had texted, Snapchatted, replied to an Instagram story, Facebook messaged, and now had finally called her.

'I was bathing,' she answered. 'I saw the strangest thing. It was a woman's back, but also not— like a demon or a dead body, but it had like fingerprints or something, or someone's hand marked right across— with an indentation, like a ring—' but our girl was scared to finish the sentence. The hollowed breath of words she could never get out without sounding completely insane. No. She sealed her lips tight together, like a child told to keep a secret. Zip her lips and throw away the key.

'Are you quite finished? I am having the worst mental health day; I simply cannot begin to function. I'm wound so tight, I could break! But anyway, the reason I'm calling is that I'm going to host one of those really truly awful parties tonight—' Lottie breathed out in ecstasy— 'the ones with death, drugs, and destruction. A party where girls go wild and the guys go nuts. Can I count you in?'

'Round up the usual suspects, and I assume you'll get your party. The whole town will be destroyed, don't you worry,' our girl spoke breathlessly. She imagined all the ways in which she could give her exactly what she wanted. *Destruction, horror, and a dash of salacious drama*, her mother's voice whispered to her. Yes, she could make that happen, just as Lottie wished. She could confront all the people in her life that had over and over again broken her down. She could finally say all the words she had swallowed over the years. Lottie wanted destruction, so she would call upon a chaos demon and hand it over to her.

Parties are the perfect place to spill other people's secrets, as everyone is locked in thin yet suffocating plastic. They watch how they speak and act as if they were characters in some noir movie. She could say a few choice words and finally be free, and with that freedom, she could be happy.

But what would she say to Lottie? She had to make sure to invite Varjack, who was a known attendant of parties like this. You see, dear reader, when she was born, she had a spirit, and it was bright orange and beautiful and demanded attention. Now, after years of labels and broken records, repeating words of all the things she was meant to be— it was safe to say she was done. And nothing could stand in her way anymore.

SEVEN HOURS

It is safe to say, dear reader, that for the first time she felt as if she had a purpose, and had concurred something. What she had started to concur was an age-old fight, one all women have been fighting. In the fifties, you see, all these women felt the same type of emptiness, a sudden overwhelming sense of nothingness. As if clothes, washing, cleaning, and keeping a tidy home should be satisfying for a sentient being who had education, thoughts, and feelings.

Betty Friedan showed us that all those housewives were having the same thought: 'She was afraid to ask even of herself the silent question— "is this all?"' We thought with careers we had won, but it changed. It pitted woman against woman which shaped the experience of women into something different than before.

That which I am trying to tell you about, something all women go through, is akin to the harshest of winters. Every woman trying to survive, alone, eyes blinded by poisonous snow. We are told to see other women as competition and as something from another world. That any woman with a thought in her brain is different from the rest of womankind. That if she has thoughts and ideas, she must be isolated in her lonely snowstorm of strangeness. This is a story of the winter of our femininity.

Dear reader, what may be the point of this awful narrative, who is this damn narrator, and why do they insist upon calling me 'dear'?

Of course, you may have already asked yourself that. You may have previously thought that over and over again, and every time I spoke to you, carefully placed my voice in your ear much like the male voice of the patriarchy does, trying to gain access to the inside to control you as you begged to know who I am. Or, you have put down the paper which carries my voice to you and in that sense, I thank you. If you do not enjoy something, I beg you not to do it. I *implore* you.

I too have known the consequences of someone else wanting something from you so incessantly it begins to feel as if your belly is filled with rocks. The guilt of daring to say no weighs you down until you can barely stand. So you finally say yes, and the rocks just become heavier.

Please do not assume I have been filled with rocks, but any woman who really trusts you will relay to you a moment where they have felt like this. As if 'no' has not been a word in their vocabulary, and the weight in their gut is almost the same as the weight of the person on top of them.

What I will tell you about myself, dear reader, is this. When I was young, and my body went through changes and became a woman's body, I learnt that respect would be given to me only if I were 'not like other girls.' I thought when those words were uttered to me that it meant something special and right. I even cursed my name, the only name given to me by a woman, for naming me after the moon. Our female ruler, controlling the tides within us. See how deep, dear reader, the hatred goes.

What the comment of 'you aren't like other girls' actually means is that they have an expectation that other women are not interesting or unique. By believing that statement and carrying it into my womanhood, I placed into my soul a patriarchal hatred for other women. I thought I was special and better and therefore not a woman, because I had *interests*. I would laugh alongside the rape jokes in fear of being called a bitch. I was better than any girl who liked makeup or bath bombs, or the girls who played with dolls and their bedroom walls were painted pink.

The night I saw the death of a pretty girl that I had written off as shallow and silly because the patriarchy demands that's how we see them, the path I was heading down changed. I saw something in the still, open eyes of her silent body. I saw the same loneliness and pain I had endured. I saw it all. I saw the way everyone in her life had let her down. I saw the way every woman had been let down. At that moment, I realized the truth of the experience of all women: we have been put into an endless winter.

We are told that to be a woman is to be inherently stupid. We are told if we are smart or unique, we do not fit the form of a real woman. This, dear reader, is *wrong*.

These words hurt me to type, but I give them to you as hope. Hope that the blood I describe will wash away the snowy poison from your eyes as it did for me. Dear reader, I pass you the story of a girl without a name, whose death sparked in me the realisation of the only truth.

What I give you is simple but true, the unmoving metaphor of winter and the story of a girl so alone in a world full of horrid people that what she lived could hardly be called a life. I give you the pure knowledge of what I believed before I saw her neck break like a twig. I can only hope you understand that maybe, the winter of our femininity could finally end.

I wish I could leave this story here, and not fill your eyes with such words of pain and death. I hope I could spare you as I wish she could have been spared from the hands of demons and ugly, angry people. But I cannot, as I am bound to tell this story with the most accurate words I can muster.

The show, as they say, must go on. Our girl sits on her bed, listening to music play aloud on her phone. Brushing her long hair, enjoying the sensation of it being pulled away from her body, and then it gently falling back into place. She may not know it, but her life, her life, dear reader, is rapidly drawing to a close.

Brush, *swish*. Brush, *swish*. Brush, *swish*.

Seven more hours for our dear girl, and she continued to brush her hair, unaware.

SIX HOURS

She sat down in front of the vanity mirror. Its cream countertop was covered in little bottles of beige and brushes stained with bright eyeshadow. Her lipstick collection stood like soldiers, ready for the battle ahead. The warmth of the bath had made her skin feel like home again. *A fleeting feeling,* she told herself, while brushing through her eyebrows. The motion relaxed her but she could still feel the butterflies in her stomach, thinking about what would happen later. She stretched her eyelid with one hand and glided black liquid across it with the other. Her mind was on autopilot with this ritual she had done so many times, ever since she was young. Her hands knew where the products went, and they did it without command.

What will tonight be like? Will it all go as planned? And if so, what will I do tomorrow? A plan hatched in her mind. She would take herself for a big meal. She would sit and eat without anyone else, in public, without putting earphones in.

Tomorrow, she would delight in taking up space. Tomorrow, she would not cringe at the thought of getting in someone's way. As she thought of all the places she would like to go on a day which you and I, dearest reader, know will never come. Her stomach rumbled, like the release of thunder after it had been built up under hot and humid air.

But she did not want to eat, for the dress she wanted to wear did not leave space for it. The way her stomach would prod out, boasting of its fullness, horrified her. *I can cut off everyone in my life, but I cannot do it looking full.* She dabbed powder under her eyes, to hide how little sleep she had gotten. *Do I feel happier when there is nothing in my stomach?* This thought made her still her hand in midair, her eyes trapped on herself in the mirror.

Well, do you? That was her mother's voice, who had always hit the end of questions solidly as if it was never really a question at all.

Memories of watching her mother stare into a mirror pulling on different areas of her body were brought into her mind. The dinner table in her childhood home, where everyone was eating apart from her mother, who sat sipping wine instead. A sharp look when she asked for seconds. A ban on sweets. A ban on carbs. *I feel more like you when I haven't eaten,* she replied to her mother's voice, but there was no answer.

No, screw it, she thought, *today is the day everything changes, not tomorrow.* She grabbed her phone, ordering from a local takeaway. It would arrive in twenty minutes.

She remembered a time when Ed and Lottie had broken up at midday. By five o'clock she was in his bed naked and pretending to orgasm. He had traced the lines on her belly that came when she hit puberty. She took this as an act of adoration until he propped himself up on one arm and told her he saw an advert for a cream to get rid of those things.

He told her she just needed to stop eating lunch, just eat two meals a day, and then your body will go into starvation mode and you'll lose weight. She told him that she liked lunch because of all the options she could have.

He scrunched his nose at this. 'We all have to make sacrifices, don't we?'

Looking back she wanted to punch him for it, and she smiled to herself. *I will get my revenge tonight.*

The food arrived, a large burger and salty chips. It looked greasy, shining in the soft lighting of her bedroom. *Soft lighting reduces the appearance of cellulite,* Lottie had told her, with a look on her face like she could laugh at any moment. She held a single chip between her fingers, and it was chunky and brown at its edges. It reminded her of lunch with her grandparents, sitting on the beach in some seaside town. It reminded her of a time when food wasn't the enemy, when she had no enemies at all.

She puts it in her mouth, the salty softness crushed between her teeth. She swallowed it into an empty stomach, and it felt good. A warmth came about her, filling up her fingers as she bit the food, her bites growing bigger and bigger.

Just as it had arrived, it quickly disappeared into her. She looked up, catching herself in the mirror. There was a grease stain smeared across her cheek. There was food between her teeth. She took a deep breath. *This is okay. I'm okay.*

A panic arose in her. A pricking sensation on the back of her scalp, along her forearms, and all over her greasy fingers. Then there was nothing, she felt nothing as she got up, and walked down the hall to the bathroom. Running the water so none of her housemates could hear her. As quickly as it had arrived, as quickly as it had gone down, so it came back up.

She stood, feeling hollow once again. *Hollow is safe. Like a perfect doll. You are my perfect doll,* her mother's voice whispered to her. She stared out the window in the hallway, trying not to look at herself. She saw a magpie, hopping from one branch to another. Only one, one for her sorrow. She nods, acknowledged its presence, and she felt the sorrow from the bird soak her bones. Fully gone was the girl who stood in a mirror admiring herself. She felt like a complete stranger to that girl. Now, all she felt like was a sack of bones with nothing special underneath them at all.

She had to get dressed, she had to get going. Tonight would be the night everything would get better. Today, she told herself, would be the last day she felt bad about herself. Tomorrow when she woke up, everything would feel like a movie again— and she would be the star.

But what to wear? What would she feel confident in? What would make people's heads turn in the right way, in a way that would make them convinced she was an image of perfection so she could breeze past them, acting careless and they would instantly hate themselves for not being like her, for not looking like her. And for that moment, her world would feel whole and she would feel shiny, as if she were some decadent thing that put others to shame. But what items of clothing gave that impression? How could she find something to say and do all that? She stared at the clothes in her wardrobe. Funny. None of them said anything, they all just hung there and seemed almost gruesome to her now, as she thought about how they look on her.

This one is too tight, this one rides up when she walks, this one looked good on the website but when it arrived it didn't look so effortless on her. They all seemed not good enough, not aware of the occasion at hand.

She pulled on a dress she had never worn. It hung strangely on her body and she thought the colour of it was almost mocking her. Hastily, she pulled it from her body and purposely stood on it as she went to find something else.

What if she wore jeans? Loose around the waist jeans with a tight top that made her tits jiggle just right so that even if they weren't looking her in the eye, she knew they would be looking somewhere. Would everyone else be in jeans though? Would her wearing jeans be like a drop in a denim ocean? She needed something that made more of a statement. *Not jeans,* she thought, as she threw them over her shoulder to join the dress on the already messy floor.

What about a skirt? Something short and flirty, or something long and flowy that made her look like a perfectly respectable type of person. She shook her head; a long skirt won't turn heads. A long skirt is the outfit of a wallflower she thought to herself. But a short mini skirt, that could scream 'look at me—' that could do the trick.

She picked up a red skirt with frills, something to say that she was feisty. After all, she would be causing a lot of fights tonight.

She thought about all the raised voices, all the red cheeks and maybe even slapping that could go on tonight. It made her nervous, but the kind of nervous a person gets just before fireworks go off. The thought of it all made her empty stomach dance.

The skirt looked stupid, and even worse, she didn't know what to pair it with. A t-shirt? To make the whole thing more casual? Or a strap top? Would that make it look cheap though? *Cheap and unoriginal*, she thought. *Come on!* she told herself. *Do better!* She tapped her forehead as if it would make the perfect outfit pop out of her mind and land on her body.

Go back to dresses, she told herself. *Let's look at dresses again.* A black dress, how many of those did she have? A simple, little black dress. She could pair it with strappy sandal heels, maybe a nineties inspired cardigan over the top? No. She realised, if she got there early enough, that's exactly what Lottie would be wearing. And she would rather turn up naked than turn up wearing something Lottie would wear.

She was running out of time. Panic rose in her stomach. Maybe this was a sign, she shouldn't go. She shouldn't do this. What would be the point, if she doesn't look absolutely perfect while doing it?

If it couldn't play out like a movie— if the costuming doesn't work, then the threads can be pulled apart and the once neat package of her emancipation would simply be a daydream she had once had before she fell asleep in the bath.

But then it hit her. If Lottie always wore black, she would wear the opposite. A little white dress. She could turn people's heads by looking so angelic, so whole, without needing anyone else. That's exactly what she wanted. She pulled out all her white dresses. She needed something that said dressy, but without looking like she had spent all this time picking it out.

What says casual? A white dress with black polka dots with big sleeves but a tight body? That would make everyone's heads turn.

That would make them all say something. She slipped the dress over her head, and had to fight the zipper up. It made her arm hurt to fold it in such a way. She stared at herself in the mirror. The dress was tight around her boobs, making them almost burst over the top. But she liked it. She didn't mind that it made it a little hard to breathe, in fact, it made her feel more excited. *The fireworks would be starting soon,* she told herself, and the nerves would go away and she could walk away from that house without one single regret.

No, she thought, *I won't walk away. I will skip away happily and begin a new life. To start that new life, I will burn all my clothes and never spend another second worrying about what I am going to wear.*

I am sad to say this, dear reader, although we both know it. I must address the irony of her thoughts and the bitter sadness they fill me with. She would never skip away from that house. I wonder if her soul still wanders in that now empty house, or maybe she is wandering somewhere else. Maybe heaven is real, and I must convert my religion. Maybe she is the Patron Saint of all hurt women.

She does not know that her clothes would be taken home by her parents, unwashed, and that her family members would take them out of their boxes once and a while just so they can press them to their faces and pretend that she is still alive. She does not know all these things won't come true. She doesn't know that the timer on her life has almost ended, and she doesn't know how much of that time she has wasted by trying to pick out an outfit that impresses strangers.

There is one thing, however, dearest reader of mine, that is good about this moment. She never again will have to worry about what she is going to wear.

FIVE HOURS

The party had begun, and the air hung low in anticipation. The birds sang in muted tones filled with remorse, and to anyone walking below they looked like vultures circling a dead thing. Even the skyscrapers themselves seemed to hunch over in fear of being noticed. The lights are lowered, the music moved into the ground. The party rang itself into succession.

At first, the people trickled in like a tap that can't quite turn off. They formed slow circles, holding cups poured with heavy hands. They started off by speaking in polite tones of summers, weekends, and the weather. They bobbed their heads to signal they enjoyed the music playing. They complemented each other's outfits. They held each other by the elbows and air-kissed like they're on TV. They made jokes about the internet, old people, and the inescapable death that is coming for us all. They poured drinks down their honey-lined throats. Their thrifted designer clothes were worn as a poor attempt to make well the scars their mothers and fathers left on the earth. They used bamboo cutlery and toothbrushes. They worried if the mere air they breathe is poison to their breasts, prostates. They used words like 'self-care' and 'toxic.' They have turned the mere art of conversation into a minefield of triggers.

But who could blame them? The horrors they created and destroyed with mere taps of their fingers on screens could be devastating. These are the messy children of the destroyers. They were grown in the sad recession reading about the golden roaring years of excess. They distilled in the fleeting joy of the internet.

They presented their complex existences in neat, edible bites and then wondered if they came off as boring. They laid in bed paralysed at night, as they watched their fears get bigger on the walls with the lights of every passing car.

Yes, their loneliness and their inability to simply connect with anything is a result of the hereditary diseases passed down to them. But, in their defence, the world is ending every other day, so who cares if one of them has a cigarette? They have pushed their own fears from balconies trying to turn them into smiles.

It could be possible that one of them, with all their trapped anger and pain, killed her. Pushed her with such force it snapped three ribs on her left side.

I ask you, could one of them that sipped slowly from a cup, laughed at a meme they were shown on a friend's phone, be a killer?

Oh, but these are clowns— sad, sad clowns. And I, dear reader, was one of them. I was the saddest one of the whole bunch. Our tears are not painted on our faces but forever frozen in place.

You may ask how I can tell what's in the minds of these kinds of people. How do I know the secret fears that grow so big in their minds, that nothing else can survive? How do I know what they cry at, what they laugh at?

Because, dear reader, I saw it all while I rolled cigarettes for tipsy, shallow girls who never bought their own baccy. My own voice, like all the others, was desperate to scream and useless to the stopping of the waves.

She entered the party, pushed open the door with one hand, the other carefully patting her hair to make the wild wispy ones conform to the majority. Her feet pushed through the threshold into warm, sweaty party air, and then everything clicked. She could feel the buzz of energy as soon as she entered. She moved like butter through the crowd.

They knew her. They all did. The boys dressed as men and the women dressed as girls all know the whispered delights that come from hot breaths about the girl who slept with both the professor and his wife. Well, the last bit was a lie. But when she had heard it at the last party, it sounded so daring and cool that she wanted to be the girl who did such things. So, she let everyone believe it was true. That had been the girl that she was, but the woman who entered the party had changed.

'Oh hey,' Ed said, seeing her from across the room. He wore dark baggy jeans, and a baggy button-up shirt that smelled faintly of the mouldy plates he had under his bed.

'Hey Ed,' she said rather bluntly, so as to hopefully not strike up a conversation.

Ed, however, was not the type of guy to pick up on any sleight of hand and hardly ever paid attention to the body language of women unless he was interested in fucking them. Of course, he *was* interested in fucking her, so his inability to tell if she was interested or not only spoke more to his utter stupidity.

'Did you hear all those cult rumours going around?' he asked, not waiting for an answer before he spoke once more, the words crashing into each other as he continued, 'Yeah it's like some stupid eighties movie, people think their lives are really gonna get better because of a human sacrifice? That's like murder, ya know? But I hear they're after a virgin, so a slut like you would be alright.'

She stared at him, confounded by the stupid look on his face. His unplucked eyebrows knitted together, his greasy hair moving slightly in front of his forehead. *How the hell are we friends?* she wondered. *How the hell did I ever think you were interesting?*

'Ed.' She smiled genuinely for the first moment since she had opened the door. 'Do you ever get tired of hiding all your intentions under slang you stole from other cultures? We all know you go home at Christmas to a southern country house and horses. That's okay. Just stop pretending to be something you aren't.'

A blush rose in his cheeks. He wasn't used to being spoken to like this. His eyes only glanced up for a second to meet hers. He took a sip of his Strongbow dark fruits, gulping it down and then muttering, 'Fuck you, bitch.'

She laughed, and walked away from him as her heart danced through her chest with glee.

'Someday a rain will come and wash all the scum off the streets!' he shouted after her, with no one turning their heads to look at him. She laughed harder at his attempt of being deep, stealing words from an old movie he hadn't even watched all the way through.

You see, once upon a time she wouldn't have dared to contradict whatever anyone had to say about her. She wanted, no she *needed*, so desperately to be thought about. She would have laughed at Ed's words and then, in a couple of hours, met up with him in the upstairs bathroom to suck him off and do drugs. It would have never occurred to her that he meant the vile words coming out of his mouth, that under the vise of his aesthetic lay a true evil.

Or do you think, dear reader, that she actually *did* know? Because it simply never mattered what they were actually saying. She was the paper doll you could dress up in whatever style or rumour you wanted. Pull the string on her back to hear her say 'yes.' Gather round to listen to the perfect girl! She will not tell you no!

A shiver went through her as she thought of the obsolete version of herself. Now, she was a woman. A person who could stand in her own power. There was no measure to be had of how sick and tired she was of all the men, and things put in place by men that tried to control her. Well, no longer. No longer.

She texted Varjack while making herself a heavy-handed drink. If she were to do this, it had to be in one grand push. All the players had to be together. She decided that she would say absolutely anything to get him to her. She could tell him she wasn't wearing any underwear. She thought, *tell him you're dripping wet just thinking about him. Tell him—*

Oh, what does it matter what she tells him? She could text a single emoji, and he would be hard in his jeans. The last thought made her laugh. *Oh God, what did I ever find so attractive about a man like that?* And her friends, her stupid friends who cared more for the parties and the followers on TikTok more than her, a real human being filled with the deepest sadness.

Dear reader, there comes a time in every party when you know the night is officially underway by the number of girls that are crying. They do this in any place that looks dramatic: the bathroom to create an extensive line, the stairs so everyone hears their snot-filled sobs wailing above the noise of the party. I do not mean to make it sound like girls do not have reason to cry. They do. The terrifying thing, dear reader, is that every girl has a reason to cry.

They all have reasons to sob their hearts out morning noon and night. The tears come in the night for a reason, however. They look around at this party, they see these men shaped like fathers and brothers and realise something hidden in the locked box deep inside the female brain, a truth that scares them to their core. The alcohol they pour in their throats reveals something about the system to them, how truly dark and scary it is, and they can barely contain it. Their bodies try to push the thoughts out through their eyes and noses until they can't see or breathe, and they wake up wondering what the hell they were crying about. They apologise to everyone they know and sit all day with an uncomfortable feeling in their chest.

That, my dear reader, is just about the most prime example I can show you, of the winter of our femininity.

THREE HOURS

Where was I? Oh yes, the girl with three small hours of life left stepped further into the labyrinth of a party. Her dress clung too tightly to her ribs, making the breath in her lungs move faster the drunker she became.

She watched the people at the party, children dressed as adults, playing with their lives like a game on their phones. A good Instagram story means a moment of relief from their burdens. These types of people, my dearest reader, are the ones I feel sorry for, but also hate.

She ascended to a higher level of party hell, up past the girl crying loudly on the stairs, and further past the couple whose sparks seem to resemble Romeo and Juliet as she took a hit off his vape pen while listening to his views on Brexit.

A bedroom door closed but there was no need to knock as she opened it. Within the room lay a multitude of arms and legs and nipples. They moaned and sighed together like a perverted orchestra of pleasure. Better yet, their appearance could be described as some kind of bee colony with their queen, who touches nothing and no one but is to be always felt. Her best friend, the ringleader. She could even be her old-fashioned pimp, minus the hat and ivory cane.

'Can I talk to you, Lottie?' her voice shattered the magic of the scene they had put themselves in. Her voice cut through the movie playing in all their heads, and they groaned in varying senses.

'I'm a little busy right now,' Lottie's voice replied back, and giggling ensued. This was not how it was meant to go, but she couldn't lose hope yet. There was still a chance.

'Now,' our girl said, before she slammed the door behind her. She leaned against the wall, waiting for Lottie to pull herself from that which she had previously been more inclined to.

She stirred her brown drink with her finger, sucking it afterward to taste the syrup off it. *This was the kind of drink you could hide something in*, she thought to herself, *a pill or a powder*. Anything could have been hidden behind the bubbling surface of the liquid. She shrugged the thought off and kept sipping.

Could this drink, dear reader, be lined with something other than vodka? Could it contain a tasteless, scentless drug that makes the pushing of someone out a window so easy, it could be done with one hand?

'Is this really necessary?' Lottie asked as she walked through the doorway, pulling her blonde hair out of the neckline of someone else's university hoodie. It struck her how perfectly young Lottie looked, how sweet and innocent a girl like this could be. For a moment, the image of her as someone with blood on their hands faded. She looked, just for a second, like a girl who was just as scared and alone as any other girl in the world.

Then the moment passed, and the steely look in Lottie's eyes sent trembles up our girl's spine.

'I have to talk to you. I can't keep doing this all the things we've—' The breath she had taken had run out. The nerves slipped up her confidence, just for a moment, but enough for Lottie to see through her. 'I think I'm cursed Lottie; everything is so hard. When I was little, the world seemed so big and colourful. And I felt... I always felt like I was big enough for it. That me and the world were perfectly sized together and I could walk through it— I could walk through it in unison. But the world has gotten bigger, and darker, and there is no more colour, only grey. And I got older, but I got smaller. I'm smaller and I am just clinging to nothing. I can feel the world spinning around me and I can't do anything but close my eyes and hold on tight for safety, I—'

'What's any of this got to do with me?' Lottie's voice, carving the air like a knife. Each word its own little sword, ripping and shredding any confidence the girl in front of her seemed to have. She thought it was funny, really, this girl who had once looked so beautiful to her. Now she could not see what had first drawn her to her, she just looked average.

'Seriously, what has this got to do with me?' Lottie repeated. 'You come here, looking like shit, at my party, trying to do what, exactly? Make me feel something for you? Again? I don't know what has gotten into you. You used to be fun. You used to be cool. I thought you were something special, but I guess I was wrong.'

'I'm losing my mind, Lottie,' she told her softly, hoping against hope for a shred of humanity. 'I see things. I have conversations with myself, I can't even keep track of my days— I don't know what I've done today. I can't tell you the hours I have wasted, and I don't even know how I wasted them. I see— I see things that aren't there. I hear my mother, that's new, a real kicker.' She realised she was rambling, and stopped talking.

'Whoopty-fucking-do! I don't see how any of this is my fault,' the words poured out of Lottie's mouth, filled with venom. 'I gave you friendship, and when you needed money I gave you a way to get it! You fucked my boyfriend behind my back every time we broke up, and now what? You want me to feel something for you? You want me to *cry* for you?'

The volume of Lottie's voice had raised, and the heads of those sat on the stairs had turned and looked away swiftly after seeing the look on Lottie's face. Aware of how she was starting to look to others, she pushed a breath out of her nose to calm herself down. 'I wouldn't cry for you even if you were dead. Do you understand me? You do not get to fuck everything up because you want more attention. I have worked too hard, and refuse to let a

41

mess like you change that. Have you got that through your thick skull?'

Our girl nodded, staring down as the speech crumpled in her hands like the petals of a rose once blushed to perfection, now aged and lined. Her carefully chosen words polished like silver had rusted right in front of her.

All she had left in her mouth was a bitter taste, and these few words: 'I loved you. I loved you like a real person loves another person. And you? You treated me like paper. A paper doll that you tore apart because you felt like it.'

The times I am lost for words, dear reader, are few, to say the least— but the look on Lottie's face as these words landed in her ear and our girl brushed past her was something made of so pure a gold my words could not describe it. Down the stairs, our girl looked back for a second to see the still frozen Lottie just starting to express emotion again. Her eyebrows furrowed together, her eyes darkened, and the look could only be described as pure hatred. A look, dear reader, that can only be described as a look an insane person might get before they commit a heinous crime.

As she walked, her feet happily skipped down the staircase until one of her shoes found its way off from the foot it clung to and found itself slipping, slipping away from all ties of life and responsibilities it had as a shoe. It tumbled its velvet body down the stairs, landing on the last step with its sole face up ready to meet its maker. She felt a redness rise to her cheek. She whipped her head around to make sure no one saw that she could not even control her shoe. She stared at the shoe for a moment before she jumped down the last two steps, placed it back on her foot, and moved through the growing thicket of people to make another drink.

You must understand, dear reader, hers was a face known well at parties. I have been privy to a few exposures of what a drink may do to this girl. Her topless table dances, her cheeks sodden with dark mascara tears; the boys and girls whose lips she kissed while a smile seemed to be stuck in her teeth. As she mixed more liquid with liquid, she allowed the voices of the group beside her to wash over her. One boy's voice, Ed's voice, spitting with stupidity, rang out above the rest.

'I'm just saying,' he said, louder than the boom of the music with his eyes grinning as he decided to play devil's advocate, 'that without offence— stupid people have kids faster than educated people.' He let out a breath, as if by saying such a stupid thing his mind was lighter for it. He laughed to himself, the kind of laugh only men had when its sound was louder than any music could ever be. 'You can disagree, but it's a fact. All kids in school now are going to be the kids of stupid, lazy chavs.'

The group around him sighed, shook their heads at him, but no one said anything. They all seemed to think that maybe he was right, or maybe they thought that with men like that— so wrapped in their own opinions they have collaged together from one conservative uncle and Jeremy Hunt— their breath is not worth being wasted on such stupidity. Ed locked eyes with her, chuckling under his breath and saying loud enough for her to hear, 'Yeah, someday a rain will come and wash all the scum off the streets.'

Her eyes rolled at his repetition, hurt to know that no one would say anything to contradict him. She sipped her drink and felt as all girls do at times— the sudden and overwhelming need to be alone. She moved away from Ed and his poisonous words.

She wandered through the party, watching the people and the bodies they inhabit. She brushes past me, bumping my shoulder. I remember frowning at her when this happened. *Did she not see me?* I wondered. *Can anyone see me?* At this time, my most lovely reader, I stretched my shoulders out only to find they felt heavy, like stone, and bustled my way out to the garden to smoke the last of my laced cigarettes.

She kept moving though, in the opposite direction of the ocean of bodies. The party had quite a good turn out; Lottie would be pleased with the sight of all the drama that had begun to splash about like white sea foam on an unsteady ocean.

She sipped her cup, finding that all the voices felt overpowering to her now. Like she could not hear herself think, like she could not hear the pinging texts arriving from Varjack. She looked for a quiet space, standing in front of a closed pine door she pressed open, to find a space filled with darkness and quiet. Perfection.

She stepped in, closing the door behind her silently so no one else would enter after her. The room was illuminated in a quiet shade of moonlight. It was a dining room, or the student version of such space. It seemed as if the space was breathing, a constant small in and out that felt oddly calming to her.

There was a long sofa, blocking half the room from her view. She could see a dining room table beyond it and to her side was a cabinet with its top covered in books with uncracked spines, from the university courses of girls who lived in the house. *Internalized Misogyny as a Moderator of The Link Between Sexist Events and Women's Psychological Distress*, read a white book with large black text against it. *What a long title*, she thought to herself. *I'm surprised that they could even fit the whole thing on the spine.*

She took a sip of her drink, and sighed softly as she felt it flow down into the empty pit of her belly. *I shouldn't have thrown up that burger*, she thought, getting angry with herself as she thought about the hunger gnawing in her. *But an empty stomach does make the dress look better.* She reached out to touch the soft shiny spines of the books.

Could she stay in here forever? You ask, dear reader, could she be safe in here until the sun rises and she lives another day, and the day after that. And the next day, could she live until she has had time to read all these books that interest her? Could she keep living, one day at a time? Until one day, all the sadness in her bones has dried up and she feels something again?

Oh, my dearest reader, I wish it could be so. If you stopped reading now, I could stop writing. You could go on pretending that this is the last page of the story in your hands and believe her heart beats on until nature makes it stop. But for those of you who want to read until the true ending of this tale, I will carry on.

She heard something now, that perhaps the thoughts in her head and the alcohol in her blood had blocked out. A soft moan, or maybe a sigh, came from the seats of the sofa. She realised she is not alone in this room. The safety of it changed in a moment, and the moonlight became sharper and the paper on the books looked ready to leave cuts all over her skin.

She was not to have known, dear reader, that five minutes before she entered the room, a couple had come in, their mouths locked together, their smiles dashing brightly. That was not the same image she received from the couple. They sat up from their reclining position on the sofa, the boy's lips stuck to the girl's neck. Her eyes darted about the room. Her hands lay down by the sides of her body.

'Maybe we should go back to the party,' she told him, and he laughed.

'You've got me all riled up now, you don't get to stop now,' he told her. Kissing her unenthusiastic lips, she sighed. He moved her hands to be around him. He told himself, *this is how it should be. This is how it always works. You just got to convince them. Tell her she wants it too.* He ordered, 'Come on baby, do it how you know I like it, be good for me.'

The girl felt something block her throat. But she said nothing as he pressed her down. She sighed louder, trying to express something to him in a language he did not care to speak. He took it as a sign she was getting into it.

'Good girl,' he whispered, stretching his arms across the sofa in a state of total relaxation.

Our girl, standing only fifteen steps from them, did not know what to say or what to do. She clung to her empty cup and stared as if she was watching a gripping scene in a movie. But it felt like an out of body experience, watching something she had seen so many times in her own life but from a different angle. Just at that moment, her phone chimed loudly.

The guy whipped his head around. 'What the fuck are you doing?' he yelled, as the girl sat back up and stared at her. '*Get out!*'

A faint trace of panic rose in him. *What did she think she just saw? How much did she hear?*

'I'm sorry,' she said. This wasn't an out of body experience, she wasn't staring at herself but someone else. This girl's face was round, her hair was short and black, sleek in the moonlight. She could see the tearing in her eyes like she had seen in her own so many times. It was not her, but she knew what she was feeling.

To the girl, whose lips were now pressed shut to a hard line, she said, 'I'm so, so sorry.'

Our girl, finally feeling her legs again, moved out of the room quickly, back into the bright loud warmth of the party.

She felt something tighten in her chest, then loosen. Her whole body felt like dead weight. She brought her phone to her face, trying to read the technicolour screen. But the words blurred in her eyes, she was breathing too fast and swallowing down a sour taste too quickly. She closed her eyes, and pressed her free hand to her forehead.

She looked for a place she could be alone. Bathroom. She headed there, the air in her lungs entering and leaving without making a difference. *Just act normal.* She pushed past the line from the bathroom, receiving an angry, 'Hey!' as she did. She barely heard it and slammed the door shut.

She closed the toilet lid, sitting on it and trying to focus on the coldness of it. She wanted it to ground her, become the centre of gravity and keep her from floating off into the stars. But the bathroom felt as if it was swaying, ever so slightly, as if she was on a cruise ship. She closed her eyes, gently pressing her fingertips over them. They felt as if they might fall out. She tried to make the oxygen in her lungs do something to calm her down.

What is happening now inside the room? No. Don't wonder, everything is fine. Everything is fine. She wanted it. She was happy. I should have left sooner. Everything is fine, everything is fine. She's okay, I'm okay. You have a mission. You have things to do. You need to move on. She is okay.

One more deep breath with her eyes closed. *Open your eyes now.* She does. The world is still rotating.

There's a knock at the door. *You don't have to leave the bathroom until you're ready*, a soft little voice told her. She placed her hand over her heart. *Jesus Christ, why is it beating so fast? I saw nothing. Nothing was happening. You're overreacting.*

She stood up, pulled her dress down from where it had ridden up. She looked at herself in the mirror. She had slightly smudged the careful eyeshadow she had done hours ago, but apart from that, she looked fine. In fact, dear reader, she looked better than fine. She looked put together. She did not look like anything less than perfect.

Something about looking in the mirror made her feel worse. *You know why you're crying*, the little voice told her, *because at every other party you would have been that girl feeling pressured into doing something you didn't want to do.*

A tear slid down her cheek. She looked down into the sink to avoid meeting her own gaze. The door slammed open, another girl falling into it. They made eye contact; the drunk girl was clinging onto the doorknob as if it was a life preserver.

'Hi,' said the girl, 'I'm sorry, I just really have to pee and the door wasn't locked so I just turned it— wait, what's wrong, are you okay?' She saw the path the tears had taken down the cheeks of our girl.

'Oh, I'm fine. I'm done in the bathroom now. You can have it,' our girl said, gathering her things together.

'Thanks, are you sure you're okay?' the other girl said, her words slurred together slightly as if they were all one very long word. Our girl nodded, passed her to rejoin the party, and disappeared into a sea of people.

Dearest, most beloved reader, I spoke to the drunk girl after the party, and what she told me I will reveal to you now. She told me she felt off for the rest of the party, something gnawing in her gut that maybe if she had one less drink she could have managed to say something meaningful. She told me she had left the party before the death, but when she awoke the next morning and read the series of texts from all her other friends who had stayed, she wasn't surprised. She felt as if she already knew it had happened.

What would have happened if she had found the right words, I do not know. That my dearest reader, would be speculation. And I, a picture of melancholy, can only handle the facts, as I have told you before. But as the night grows darker; we arrive slowly but surely like the ticking of a clock, at the unfortunate death of a lonely girl.

Leaving the bathroom, she shook herself out of her sadness but she still felt restless.

Read the text, you idiot, she told herself sternly. He texted the same thing five times, each text two minutes apart.

A cold steel took over her heart. She knows what she has to do as she walks out into the night sky. Varjack was outside, and she wanted— no she *needed* this to go well. She knew the lines, and now she was filled with something she could not identify as the girl's teary eyes from the room filled her mind.

ONE HOUR

She walked out of the house and down the road with the still darkening twilight of summer behind her. Isn't it funny how long it takes the sun to set in the summer wind? The winter sun disappears quickly, but the summer one loves to lay about.

She looked up; the stars seemed so bright they seemed to tell her that everything would be okay. She was so distracted by the stars. She had not seen the people on the street, who mulled about like wine on a busy night. She had not noticed the ones who anxiously peeled off their red nail polish, waiting to see who got in their husband's cars.

This, by all accounts, would be the perfect night for some people. She could imagine lazy lovers staring up at the night sky and making wishes on stars. She ached for such love, but she knew she would never have it. The knowledge made her heart heavy, as she pulled open the door of his car and climbed into the seat next to Varjack.

The wife, *his* wife, who had been watching them, realized that this was the girl her husband had been cheating with and felt a bitter taste rise in her mouth as she ground her teeth together.

Our girl's pensive, dreaming state faded as she looked at Varjack. His lips pursed, expecting a kiss from her, which— knowing what she was about to do— gave the moment a sense of pure irony. Realizing that was not how he would be greeted, he looked at her, and an intensity so unique hung around her like the planets orbiting the sun.

'What's wrong?' he asked her, unable— even with all his brains— to identify it himself.

'Everything,' she replied. She clipped the word short.

'Do you want to talk about it?' he asked. He hoped for an even shorter two-letter reply. He had hoped to fuck her tonight, but her tanned legs pressed together with her knee pushed so hard against the door that it would leave a small red mark told him she was not hoping for the same. She, for the first time, looked scared of him.

She pushed a breath out from her lungs, letting it whiz past her teeth. 'You don't love me, do you?'

He paused, and sat back in the driver's seat a little more. 'I—' he started, but she held her hand up to stop him.

'I'll answer for you. You don't, you just liked me. You liked that I was an empty thing you could pour into. I was an empty canvas for you to dump expired paint on. You liked having my mouth around your dick, you didn't want to hear what I had to say. You liked that I made you feel young and important while you fucked me, listening to music you listened to when you were in school when everything felt like you had a future.

'You're sick and twisted. I've seen the pictures of your beautiful wife and kid, and you hate them, don't you? You hate them because they need you, which is why you came looking for me because wanking into a tissue didn't make you feel the same. Which was all we ever did by the way; you wanked into me and threw me to the side.

'But I convinced myself that you were interesting. I made you into a Greek god, but you're *nothing.* You're a rat. You thought I made you something cool, but it just means you're more twisted than you care to admit. What do we have in common? When have we ever shared anything more than crappy sex? Do you even know my middle name? No. You don't. Because I'm not real to you. I stop existing the moment I leave you. You might think of me like a doll, but I'm not.

'I've got a meeting with your head of department; I'm going to tell her everything. About you, about the sick way you think about your students, how we fucked in your office. And then I'm going to tell your wife. I am going to ruin you. I'm gonna fuck you over like all the times you fucked me.'

And with that, she opened the car door. His large hand wrapped itself around her elbow, the lock of his jaw set like stone. She pulled her arm free and slammed the car door behind her. Dear reader, I can only say that if she looked back, she would see that he had gotten out of his car and with a pure sense of calm, the cogs of his mind turning to create a plan.

But she started to speed walk back to the house, the sky having turned pitch black. A laugh escaped her lips, manic and cackling, unlike any sound she had ever made before. Then, it seemed that all the air in the world was gone; she walked faster, the world so dense and lacking breath, her lips moving like a fish out of water. She couldn't breathe.

THIRTY MINUTES

She ran up to the house, moved past the front door and up the stairs. She pushed crying girls and laughing boys out of the way, to the back bedroom where French doors led to a balcony.

There, her body crumpled to her knees, and she grasped the iron frame; her bright white knuckles held onto it. The contact of the cold metal began to cool down her skin. She had not noticed how warm she had been. Finally, she was able to take a breath, so deep into her lungs, it made her cough when it came back up. How odd of the air to instantly return to the earth once she was on the second story of the house. She slowly regained the ability to stand.

She began to get up, and realised how short the balcony was. Something deep in her gut begged her to head back inside, away from the groaning noises of the darkened city. But something had caught her eye, like a ring in a jewellery case. She had never seen the city skyline look so black. She wondered, *what would it be like to hang there? In the air so dark and just be wrapped up in the wind?*

Now intoxicated by the sky and all the lines it held, dear reader, she was unable to hear the party downstairs or if there were footsteps behind her. The night sky was calling to her, and she had picked up the receiver. She felt like that was where she was meant to be. There, caught in the black night sky where pain and people could not reach her. Where she would finally be safe. She felt the millions of hands push her, all the truth and lies and pain. She felt first her feet slip. She felt the air grab her from the force that pushed her from behind, with all the strength of two hands filled with hatred.

Everything in that moment felt firm, that to leap through the deep black simmering night air was where she wanted to be. She no longer felt the loneliness of life. The last breath left her; the wind had her now. She began to feel herself falling, like Alice down the rabbit hole. Her mouth opened like a rip in a canvas but let out nothing but a silent hot breath.

When she landed, dear reader, I was standing outside smoking. Staring through glass doors at a party at a world I did not feel a part of. When she landed, dear reader, the *crack smack popping* sounds of bones sounded like heavy rain, waking me out of my stares, and there lay a girl so beautiful and perfect she looked like a sleeping princess. Then I saw her open eyes, full to the brim of horror and pain. Then the blood poured out slowly to fill the gaps between the slabs of the patio. Then her hair changed its colour, matted by blood, and the metallic scent filled the air. Then the crowd came out, the music cut. We all took her in as a painting hung on the wall of a gallery. Then came a feeling of hot coals being shoved in my throat, and I recognised it as heavy sobs.

When she landed, dear reader, I looked upon the faces of the players that surrounded me. I saw her hand outstretched, pointing only into the distance when I wished it would point to the one who did it. This beauty, who I had judged and mocked from afar, whose name I did not know but whose sorrow was as deep as mine, now lay before me dead. All the actors gathered, feigned sadness and disgust. The boys showed their gums, and the girls showed their tears. The ambulance wailed white noise for the death of another woman. I begged the body to tell its story, but the air had left its lungs.

Dear reader, I ask you if you know. If you can take my half-truths, my rambling sentences and report back to me an answer, of who or what killed the girl who woke me like the whistling foehn over the cold alps, from the winter of our femininity.

Acknowledgements

I consider myself a very lucky person. I have lots of people in my life who instantly come to mind when I think of who I could thank. My mother, my father, my boyfriend, friends, even the co-workers at my old job. The blessings I have received are plentiful and I am in constant awe that I have anyone in my life that can put up with me and my fun facts for more than five minutes. When one has experienced trauma in life, it makes you even more aware of the good moments. When my boyfriend holds me in his arms, I am aware of the moments I spent alone, hurting myself as a teenager. When I get to laugh with my friends, I think of all the moments I have cried with them. I, like most of those who contain a poetic soul, am constantly looking for metaphors, similes and juxtaposition in my memories and experiences.

To sit down and write an acknowledgements page is a strange sensation. I wonder about all the things that have led me here, all the things I have overcome. I was a strange child, born into traumatic settings and destined, it seemed to spend most of my life explaining away an extra last name. Which is why, I do not write with a last name attached to me. I am my own person; my words are my own and to assign them to anyone but me would be a heart wrenching level of betrayal. Therefore, I will write simply with the first two names my mother gave me, that is enough.

The first person I should acknowledge then, to work chronologically through my life, would be my mother. A woman who bore me through the trauma of birth and then the trauma of my biological father abandoning us. I was raised in her image, a stoic woman with a strength so bright like the sun you might want to wear sunglasses. The woman who gave me her face and her double jointed elbows, a woman who I would be lucky to end up like.

My siblings, Stephanie and William. Headstrong and powerful people, the backbone of my life. My grandparents, Bill and Maureen whose love for each other inspires my poetry constantly. My grandfather was my first storyteller, he could paint pictures so frightening with his words that me and the rest of my cousins would scream at the sound of the wind through the trees.

Last but not least would be the man who became my father, Gary. His passion, his stubbornness, and his love for me made me feel like the most special girl in the world. There will never be enough words to thank him for everything he has given me, when I give so little back.

My friends, who after ten years of friendship feel more like siblings. They are, as I have called them in previous stories, the blanket that keeps me warm in autumn. Stars in a navy sky. I want to thank you all for the moments you have given me, either in woe or joy— I had the time of my life growing up with you. I am proud of the wild women you have all become.

I am extremely thankful to all my English teachers throughout secondary school— Mrs. Morgan, Mrs. Hall to name a few— who helped me realise I did actually have a talent for something. To my university lecturers (especially Dr. Nicolas Duffy, Karen Solie, Rachid M'Rabty, Dr. Sonja Lawrenson, and Joe Stretch) who watched me flourish from someone who had never written a poem once in her life to someone who could write a whole book of them. You all collectively created my north star, a love of literature, which guides me when I am lost.

My university friends, without whom I never would have survived and who have made Manchester not only where I live but have made it my home. I love you all dearly, and cannot see what you do in life because I know it will be spectacular. My old housemates, Dan and Nastasha, who turned a mould infested student house into my safe space.

The love of my life, Zachary, who when he met me six years ago fell in love with someone utterly lost and heartbroken. You believed in me when I didn't, you helped me achieve everything I wanted to and more. You have given me the life I have always wanted and the adventure I could have only dreamed off. You are the reason I can understand the love songs, the sonnets, and the prose.

There is one person left to thank, without whom this story would not contain its sadness; the girl I was at fourteen. The girl who screamed so loud but no one heard her. My only hope for this story is that someone can read it and not feel as alone as I once did. To pass on the knowledge that while the rocks at the bottom are dark and slippy, you will reach the surface.

Once again thank you, to all who I have mentioned and those I probably have forgotten. To the person who discovered coffee, to the person who threw the party where I got this idea.

Mostly to the amazing publishers who read my work and changed my life forever; I thank you from the bottom of my heart.

Thank you— from the bottom of my heart, to every single person who reads this.

About the Author

Activist, poet, and author Hellena Jane was born in Nottinghamshire 1998, to mother Teresa Mason and father figure, Gary Burns. Hellena Jane grew up loving books, movies, and storytelling. She went to school in the small town of Southwell where she met some of her lifelong friends and experienced things that helped develop her passion for justice and her emotive melancholy writing style.

She left in 2017 to go to Manchester Metropolitan University, studying in English Literature and Creative Writing. The idea for this story struck her at a house party as her shoe came off while she was walking downstairs and bugged her for a year before becoming her dissertation. During the 2020 pandemic, she expanded the text into the novella you are now holding.

Hellena Jane lives with her long-term boyfriend, Zachary, in Manchester. She enjoys large cups of coffee, thrift shopping, disposable cameras, embroidering, and spending hours explaining to her boyfriend why they should adopt a black cat.

Find her on social media on numerous accounts below:

Personal Instagram – @hellena.jane
Poetry Instagram – @poetrybyHJ
Twitter – @_WrittenbyHJ